Grandpa's Visit

Story by
Richardo Keens-Douglas

Illustrations by
Frances Clancy

Annick Press
Toronto • New York

Cover design by Sheryl Shapiro.

Annick Press Ltd.

Annick Press gratefully acknowledges the support of the Canada Council and the Ontario Arts Council.

Canadian Cataloguing in Publication Data
Keens-Douglas, Richardo
Grandpa's visit

ISBN 1-55037-489-3 (bound) ISBN 1-55037-488-5 (pbk.)

I. Clancy, Frances. II. Title.

PS8571.E454G63 1996 jC813'.54 C96-930193-6
PZ7.K445Gr 1996

The art in this book was rendered in pencil crayon on gesso.
The text was typeset in Usherwood.

Distributed in Canada by:
Firefly Books Ltd.
3680 Victoria Park Avenue
Willowdale, ON
M2H 3K1

Published in the U.S.A. by Annick Press (U.S.) Ltd.
Distributed in the U.S.A. by:
Firefly Books (U.S.) Inc.
P.O. Box 1338
Ellicott Station
Buffalo, NY 14205

Printed and bound in Canada by
Quebecor Printing Inc.

For my dad.
Always believe in the magic of life.

– Richardo Keens-Douglas

To Tess and Adam, my children.

– Frances Clancy

Jeremy was a beautiful Christmas baby, and his parents wanted to call him Jesus.

Their neighbour said it was a lovely thought but not a good idea. And because he was a wise friend, they called the baby Jeremy. Still, the parents wanted to raise the baby the way Jesus would have been, with a lot of love and care.

Jeremy was growing up to be a normal child.

He was miserable, he was funny,

he was happy, he was sad,

he was eating, he wasn't eating,

he was dirty, he was clean,

he broke an arm, he broke a window,

he bruised a knee,

he was up, he was down,

he was in, he was out.

They were a happy family.

No one knows exactly when or how it happened, but everything changed. Suddenly the parents had two jobs each. They owned every appliance you could think of. The toothbrushes were automatic and the can opener had its own room. The parents were re-carpeting this and wallpapering that, and by the time Jeremy was seven he had his own TV, video cassette recorder, computer and stereo set, and his own phone by his bed, right next to the teddy bear.

Most days Jeremy would return home from school, lock himself in and go straight to his room to play with "Tellie", the TV, and "Victor", the VCR. No friends were allowed in the house when no one else was home. No one else ever was.

Then one evening, out of the blue, the doorbell rang and standing in the middle of the entrance was Jeremy's grandfather, with the biggest smile you have ever seen and a missing front tooth.

This grandfather Jeremy had never met before. This grandfather lived far away, in another country. This grandfather was 84, looked like 74, and moved like a 64-year-old. Everybody was happy to see him. It had been so long, and all of a sudden, like a nice hot bowl of cereal on a cold day, there he was.

"Ah don't have to get an invitation to come see family. Ah just decided to come and here I am," he said. "So how is everybody doing?"

"Dad! Come on in, man. What a nice surprise," shouted the father.

"Grandpa, you look well—just in time for dinner," said the mother, and Grandpa sailed into the house.

Grandpa is the kind of fellow everybody would like to grow up to be. "Think positive and grow old doing what you love to do." That's Grandpa. A man who loves life.

Grandpa brought a little something for everybody.

Jeremy's gift was wrapped in a pretty-coloured paper, and the way that fluffy bow was sitting on top of the box like the Queen of Sheba you could tell that gift was wrapped with a lot of love and care. But Jeremy didn't notice. He just wanted to see what was inside the box. The ribbon started to fly and the large, fluffy bow went right out the window. Jeremy opened the lid, his eyes sparkling with excitement. Then he looked up at his mother and said, "But it's just a ball, Mom." He took it out of its box, and it was beautiful. He started to shake it close to his ears, expecting to hear something special.

Then he began to inspect it like an immigration officer going through a passport. Grandpa looked on, a little puzzled, but found it rather interesting.

Jeremy looked up. "Is this a secret ball-radio, Grandpa?"

"A secret ball-radio?" Grandpa said. "No, my son. It's just a simple ball—to bounce."

"Oh, I see," Jeremy said. "A simple ball—to bounce. Thank you anyway, Grandpa." And he got up, went straight to his room and played with his friends, Tellie and Victor.

Grandpa just smiled and let it pass. He knew some children have a creative way of showing happiness. But later that evening, Mom took Jeremy aside and said, "Grandpa has come a long way to meet you, young man. He had to save a lot of money to do it. Let's show a little appreciation."

But the following week Grandpa was in for a lesson and a half in truth. When the father was in, the mother was out, and when the mother was in, the father was out, and when Jeremy ran in the door, he made straight for Tellie and Victor. When the mother and father were both in, they were out like a light. Tired.

Rushing out the door one day the father said, "You know, Dad, we haven't really talked about the folks back home, but we will, we will. There's a good programme on channel six this morning. I'm sure you'll enjoy it."

Grandpa felt that the TV wasn't all that great, except to put a vase of flowers on. So one night he left them all watching Perry Mason and the judge in the courthouse, and strolled into Jeremy's room. He was amazed: an electronic dinner buffet.

And Grandpa became curious enough that he decided to help himself. He started with the P's. He PRESSED, PUSHED and PULLED, and all of a sudden there seemed to be 5000 "bees" in the room: *Bzzzzzz,* BOing and BOOOMMM, then—a Black-out.

Everything crashed: computer, video and clock. Even the dishwasher in the kitchen stopped its spinning. The house was in darkness.

Jeremy's father shouted, "—and Perry Mason was just about to win his case."

Poor Grandpa. He got so nervous he ran out of the room and said, "Maybe it's just a little fuse dat blow..."

The mother said, "'Maybe a little fuse dat blow', Grandpa. You mean a few fuses."

Well, Grandpa had blown every fuse in the fuse-box. So they lit a few candles, and they were all sitting down in the living room together, but nobody said a word, as if in mourning for their appliances.

Then Grandpa noticed the ball, forgotten in a corner. He went and picked it up. "Jeremy, catch!"—and he threw the ball at Jeremy.

Jeremy caught it, looking quite surprised. "Here, Grandpa," he said, throwing it back, and Grandpa caught it and threw it to Dad, who caught it and threw it to Mom. She caught it and threw it to Jeremy. They played catch for the very first time, and by candlelight. There was a smile on everybody's face. Then Grandpa said, "Let's play Donkey."

Jeremy asked, "How do you play Donkey?"

Grandpa said, "You mean you never played Donkey? My father taught me how to play it as soon as I could spell, and I taught your father when he was a little boy. Light another candle." And Grandpa started, "Every time you drop the ball, you get one letter in the word 'donkey'. The first who spells the whole word is the big donkey."

You should have seen them dive for that ball in the candlelight. They were under the table and in the kitchen, Dad with a spin like a ballet dancer, then the mother, running to catch the ball, tripping on the fluffy carpet and throwing it to Grandpa, who missed the ball, and while Grandpa was diving he banged into the TV. The screen cracked.

They all stopped and looked at the TV. Then everybody was on the floor, laughing and laughing. They had not had such a good time horsing around together since Jeremy was a very small boy. Grandpa looked at them in the candlelight and smiled, and his heart sang.

Then, suddenly, Dad had replaced the fuses in the basement and the lights came on. Everyone said sadly, "Aww—"

Grandpa stayed another week. They talked around the dinner table, they walked together, played ball at the park—and Grandpa even learned a few video games.

As they waved goodbye to Grandpa, they all knew it had been a visit they'd always remember. "It was really great having Grandpa," said the mother.

"Yes, we've been missing so much," said the dad.

"Can we go visit Grandpa?" asked Jeremy.

"We sure will, son, and real soon."